P9-DBL-911

Bear about Town
Oso en la ciudad

Stella Blackstone
Debbie Harter

Barefoot Books
Celebrating Art and Story

HONEY HOUSE
CASA DE LA MIEL

Bear goes to town every day.

Oso va a la ciudad
todos los días.

He likes to walk all the way.

Hasta allí
le gusta caminar.

BAKERY

On Mondays,
he goes to the bakery.

Los lunes,
va a la panadería.

On Tuesdays,
he goes for a swim.

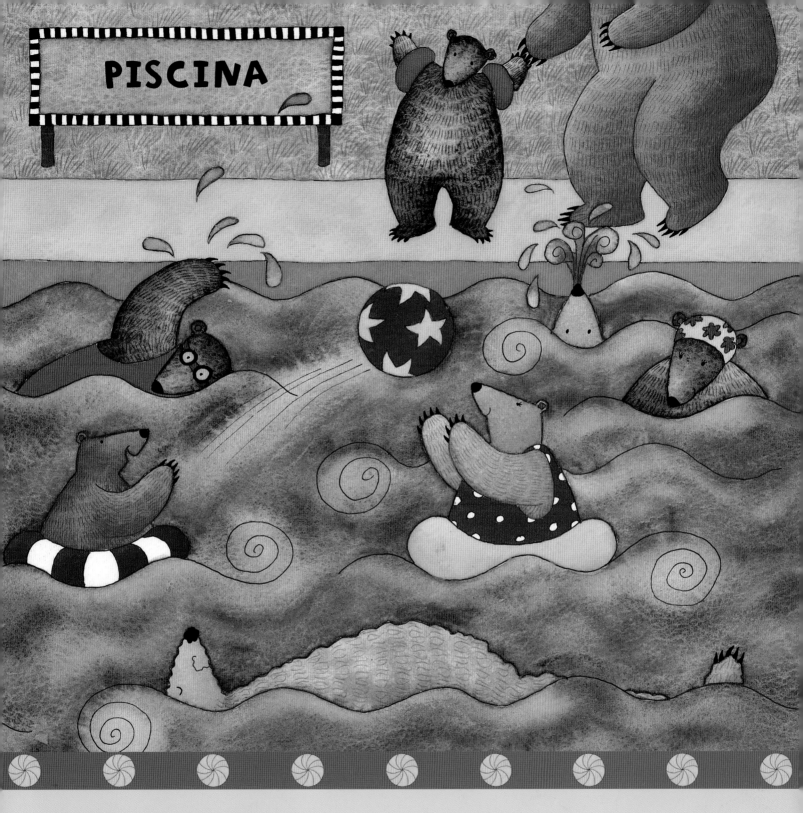

PISCINA

Los martes,
va a nadar.

On Wednesdays, he watches a film.

Los miércoles,
ve una película.

**On Thursdays,
he visits the gym.**

Los jueves,
va al gimnasio.

On Fridays,
he goes to the toyshop.

Los viernes,
va a la juguetería.

On Saturdays,
he strolls through the urk.

PARK • PARQUE

**Los sábados,
va al parque a pasear.**

On Sundays,
he goes to the playground,

Los domingos,
va al patio de juegos.

And plays with his friends until dark.

Y juega con
sus amigos hasta la oscuridad.

Find the places
Bear visits each day.

Busca los lugares que Oso visita cada día.

Vocabulary / Vocabulario

Monday – lunes

Tuesday – martes

Wednesday – miércoles

Thursday – jueves

Friday – viernes

Saturday – sábado

Sunday – domingo

Barefoot Books
124 Walcot Street
Bath, BA1 5BG, UK

Barefoot Books
2067 Massachusetts Ave
Cambridge, MA 02140, USA

Text copyright © 2000 by Stella Blackstone Illustrations copyright © 2000 by Debbie Harter
Translated by Vicky Cerutti

The moral rights of Stella Blackstone and Debbie Harter have been asserted

First published in Great Britain by Barefoot Books Ltd in 2000 and in the United States of America
by Barefoot Books Inc in 2000. This edition published in 2010

All rights reserved. No part of this book may be reproduced
in any form or by any means, electronic or mechanical, including
photocopying, recording or by any information storage and retrieval system,
without permission in writing from the publisher

This book has been printed in China by Printplus Ltd on 100% acid-free paper

ISBN 978-1-84686-377-6

3 5 7 9 8 6 4

British Cataloguing-in-Publication Data:
a catalogue record for this book is available from the British Library

Library of Congress Cataloging-in-Publication Data is available upon request